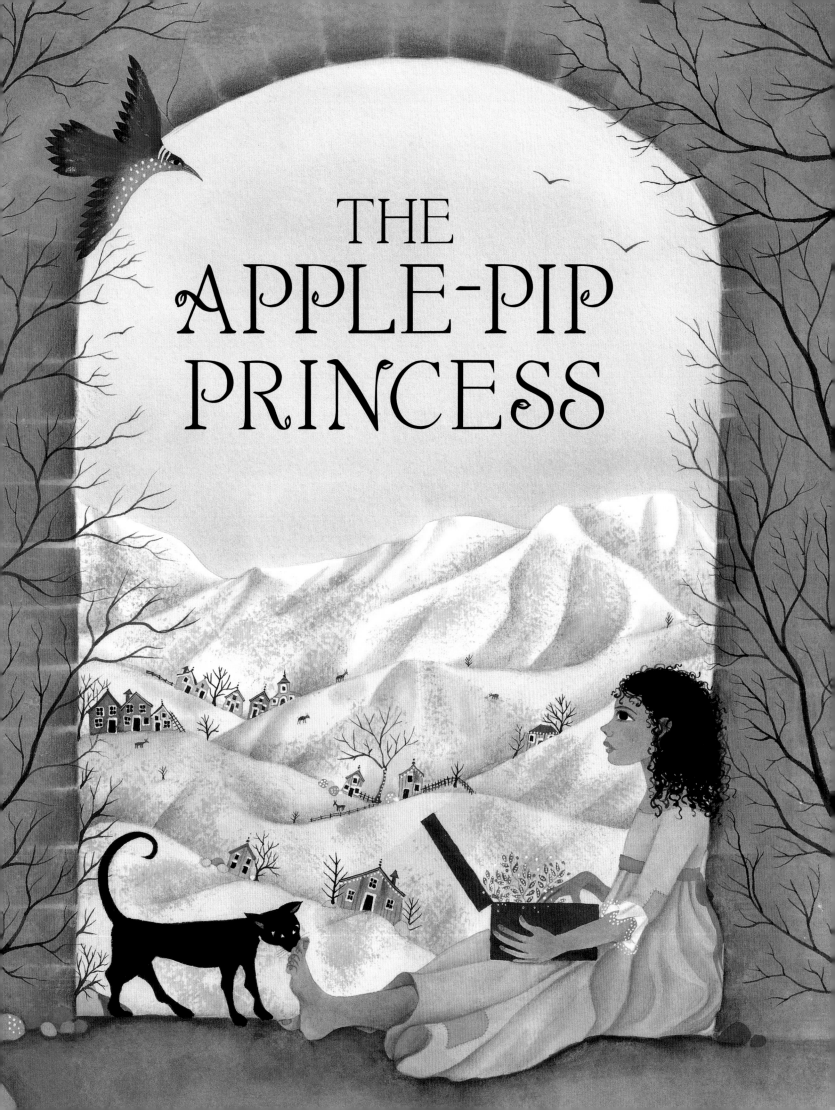

THE
APPLE-PIP
PRINCESS

For the children of Coldfall Primary School – J.R.

ORCHARD BOOKS
338 Euston Road, London NW1 3BH
Orchard Books Australia
Level 17/207 Kent Street, Sydney, NSW 2000

First published in 2007 by Orchard Books
ISBN 978 1 84616 100 1
Text and illustrations © Jane Ray 2007

2 4 6 8 10 9 7 5 3 1
Printed in China

Orchard Books is a division of Hachette Children's Books, an Hachette Livre UK company.

THE
APPLE-PIP
PRINCESS

Jane Ray

ORCHARD BOOKS

Let me tell you a story about something that happened a long time ago in a land far from here – a land ruled by an old king who had three daughters.

The kingdom had once been covered in forests filled with birdsong, and the royal palace had been a busy and bustling place. But since the Queen's death, the heart had quite gone from the kingdom – the winters were bitter, the summers were scorched and the palace was filled only with sadness. The King and his daughters had grown poor and the princesses wore patched ballgowns and had to share tiaras.

The people they ruled over were even poorer. They lived in tumbledown cottages and scratched a living from the dry earth. The children played with sticks and stones and went to bed without any supper. The animals were so skinny you could hear their ribs rattling, and the birds were too hungry to sing.

Now, before the Queen died she asked each of her beloved girls to choose one of her possessions to remember her by.

The first to choose was Suzanna, the eldest princess. Straightaway, she picked a pair of fine scarlet shoes, with heels that made sparks on the cobblestones. When Suzanna put them on, she felt tall and important.

Next came Miranda, the middle princess. She pored over the Queen's many jewels and trinkets, trying to decide what she liked best. At last, she chose a magnificent mirror made of silver and pearls. Miranda spent hours gazing into it, thinking herself quite the most beautiful princess there had ever been.

Finally, it was the turn of the youngest princess,
whose name was Serenity. She chose a simple
wooden box that she had loved since
she was a baby.

Inside the box, there were seven truly magical things that the Queen had collected when she was a little girl.

There was a scattering of raindrops, a splash of sunlight, a fragment of rainbow, a starbird's feather, a spider's dewy web, a burst of nightingale song and, right at the bottom, an embroidered silken bag that held a tiny apple pip.

Serenity liked to look
carefully through all the things inside.
They helped her remember her mother, and
of how beautiful their land had once been.

Time passed, and one day the King called his daughters to him.

"I am old now, so I must choose which of you will be the best ruler of our kingdom after I have gone," he said. "I have decided to set you a task. You must each do something to make your mark – something to make me proud of you. After seven days and seven nights, I will look at what you have done and I will make my decision."

Suzanna was clever and knew straightaway what she wanted to do.
"I will build the tallest tower in the world," she said. "It will be so
tall it will reach the moon. People will see it and remember what a
Very Important Person I am. They will be so proud to be ruled by
me that they won't mind being hungry at all."

She sent orders for people to bring all the wood in the kingdom –
even if it was the roof over their heads, or the fences that kept their
animals safe. And if anyone even thought of arguing with her, she
would have them thrown into the dark and crumbling royal dungeon!

Miranda was clever too, but rather vain and far too busy admiring herself in the mirror to have any ideas of her own.

"Right," said Miranda. "If Suzanna is building a tower tall enough to reach the moon, I will build one to reach the stars. If her tower is made from plain old wood, mine will be made of shining metal. People will see my lovely tower and remember how beautiful I am. They will be so honoured to be ruled by me that they won't mind being poor at all!"

Immediately, Miranda sent orders for people to bring her all the metal in the kingdom – everything, even their cooking pots and tin pans, copper bells and birdcages. And if anyone argued, Miranda would stamp her foot and have them thrown into the dark and crumbling royal dungeon!

Now, I expect you are wondering about
Serenity, the youngest princess. Maybe you
think that I'm going to tell you that she was
the cleverest, or the most beautiful, or her
father's favourite, because that is often the
way with fairy tales . . .

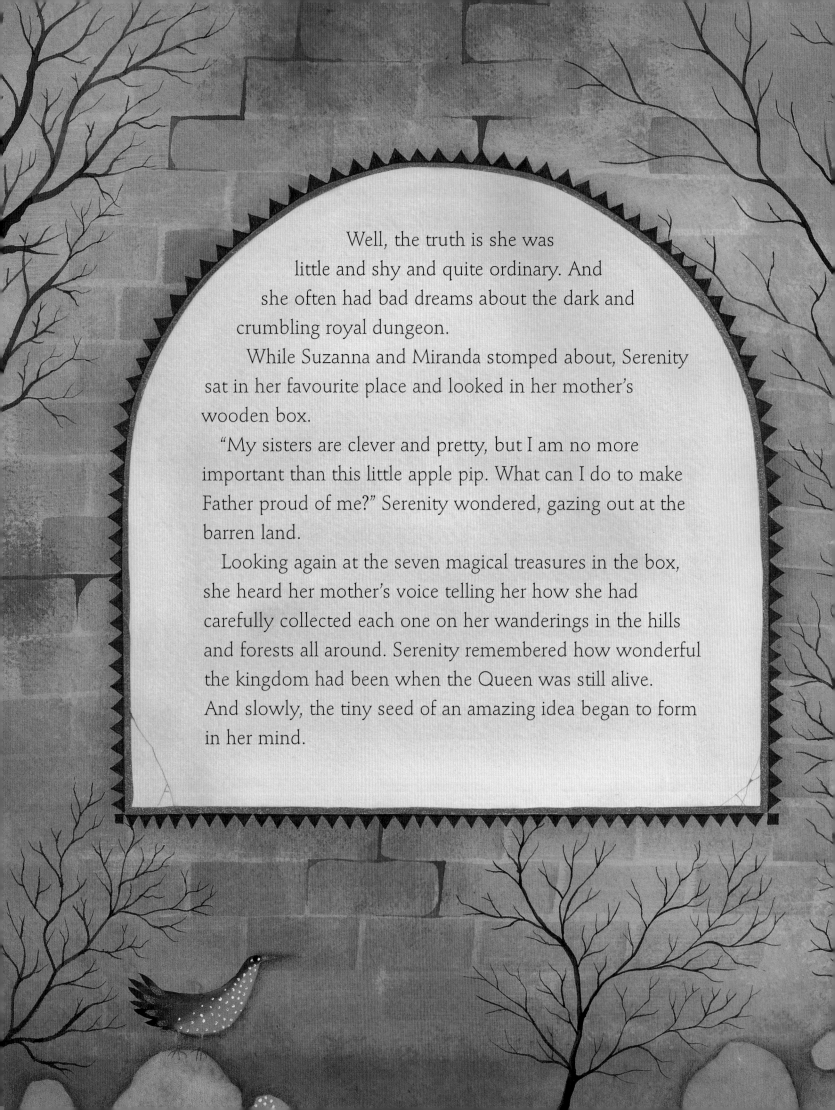

Well, the truth is she was little and shy and quite ordinary. And she often had bad dreams about the dark and crumbling royal dungeon.

While Suzanna and Miranda stomped about, Serenity sat in her favourite place and looked in her mother's wooden box.

"My sisters are clever and pretty, but I am no more important than this little apple pip. What can I do to make Father proud of me?" Serenity wondered, gazing out at the barren land.

Looking again at the seven magical treasures in the box, she heard her mother's voice telling her how she had carefully collected each one on her wanderings in the hills and forests all around. Serenity remembered how wonderful the kingdom had been when the Queen was still alive. And slowly, the tiny seed of an amazing idea began to form in her mind.

Serenity thought a while. She began to smile.
And then she began to work . . .

O n that first day, Serenity took a trowel and began to dig the
ground. It was difficult work, because the earth was baked
hard by the sun, but she kept on until there was a patch that
was crumbly and brown. Carefully, she took the tiny apple pip from
its embroidered bag and planted it in the earth.

On the second day,
Serenity dug some more
and planted the pips from
her breakfast pear next
to the apple pip. Then, she
watered them with the
scattering of raindrops.

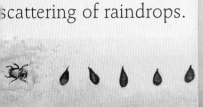

2

On the third day, she
planted the pips from an
orange she had for lunch
and let the splash of
sunlight dance over the
earth. Then, she watched
in amazement as green
shoots pushed their way
through the soil.

3

4

On the fourth day,
Serenity planted stones
from her supper-time
cherries. Then, she took
the fragment of rainbow
and flung it high into the
blue sky. The little green
plants turned their leaves
to the sun and smiled.

On the fifth day, Serenity noticed a boy from the tumbledown cottages watching her and called him over. He brought her a plum stone and began to help. They worked together all day, digging in the hot sun, and by evening they were firm friends.

Before they went home, Serenity took the starbird's feather and let it fan a soft fresh breeze over the earth.

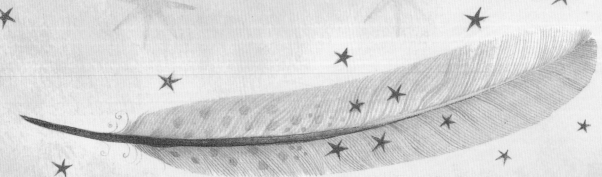

The boy's name was Joseph, and on the sixth day he returned
with olive stones from his mother. Word began to spread, and
the people came to offer gifts of orange and lemon pips.

They helped Serenity and Joseph to dig and water, to plant
and sow, and taught them all they remembered about tending
the land.

Before the sun began to set, Serenity draped the spider's dewy
web over the bright young leaves and buds of the tiny apple tree.

By the seventh day, the land beyond the palace walls was covered in the misty green of little seedlings. But Serenity had a problem . . . Although she could well imagine how lovely all the trees and plants would be when they were fully grown, she realised that they would never be ready when the King made his decision the very next day.

As evening came, Serenity suddenly put down her trowel
and looked at Joseph, at their dirty hands and muddy clothes.
   "It's no good," she said. "My father can't possibly choose me."
Joseph tried to encourage her.
   "The plants will grow," he said. "Look how strong the little
apple tree has grown. We must just be patient."

But darkness was falling and Serenity was tired and despondent. With tears in her eyes, she opened the wooden box one last time and released the burst of nightingale song among the branches of the tiny apple tree.

With the beautiful sound filling their ears,
Serenity and Joseph fell into an exhausted sleep . . .

arly next morning, the King appeared – it was time to make his decision.

Suzanna called to him from the top of her tower.

"Father, Father – look at this tower! Surely it's the tallest tower you've ever seen? I should definitely be the one to rule the kingdom!"

But the King shivered in the shadow that the huge tower cast.

"Father, Father – look at me!" called Miranda from the top of her tower. "Isn't this the most beautiful tower you have ever seen? I should rule the kingdom!"

But the King was dazzled by the shiny tower flashing in the sun.

The King looked around for Serenity, but she was nowhere to be seen. He walked out through the arch and almost tripped over Serenity and Joseph lying asleep on the ground. He woke them gently.

"Oh, Father, I'm so sorry . . ." she began, but the King took her by the shoulders and turned her around . . .

As far as her eyes could see, there were plants and graceful trees. There were fruit trees and olive trees and nut trees, all fresh and green in the early-morning sunshine. Serenity and her father walked slowly, arm in arm.

The air was full of the scent of flowers and all around them children were playing. People were picking fruit and tending the trees, and the old people were resting in the dappled shade.

The old King felt his poor unhappy heart fill with warmth again,
as all his sadness drifted away on the breeze.

"Serenity, my Serenity," he said. "You shall rule the kingdom!
For you have transformed the land and made it blossom again."

But what of Suzanna and Miranda,
I hear you ask? Well, if Suzanna stood
at the very top of her creaking tower,
on tiptoe in her scarlet shoes,
and reached as high as she could,
she could nearly touch the moon.
And if Miranda balanced on
the very top turret of her shiny
tower, she could nearly touch
the stars . . .

But after a while they
began to feel rather lonely
and noticed the sound of
laughter and birdsong
floating up on the
scented breeze.

So they climbed down and joined the King, Serenity
and Joseph, and everyone else sitting under the trees,
and they were all happy, together again.

And as day faded into night, the three princesses lay in the grass and listened to the magical sound of the nightingale's song.